TWiN Magic

Lost Tooth Rescue!

written by Kate Ledger   illustrated by Kyla May

SCHOLASTIC INC.

For Rori and Scarlett, my own magical twins!
—KL

With special thanks to Natarsha Larment, for dotting
the i's and crossing the t's. And to creative genius
Kyla May for breathing life into *Twin Magic* with
her abundant talent and impeccable style.

ISBN 978-0-545-48025-3

12 11 10 9 8 7 6 5 4 3 2 1   13 14 15 16/0

Printed in the U.S.A.   40
First printing, January 2013

Lottie and Mia are twins.
They just moved to a new house
in a new town.
Today is their first day of school.

"Hurry up, Mia," Lottie says. "It's time to go!"
Lottie's half of the bedroom is pink and messy.
Mia's half is green and tidy.

Lottie rushes out of the room.
"Wait!" Mia cries. "You forgot your lunch and your juice and your pencil case!"

"Look," Lottie whispers. "A boy!"
Lottie's too shy to say hello.
But Mia is not shy at all.

"Hi," Mia calls out.
"What's your name?"
"I'm Toby," the boy says.
"Want to walk to school together?"

In class, the twins meet
a girl named Anna.
"Hi," Anna says.
"I have a loose tooth! See?"
She wiggles her tooth.

"When your tooth falls out,
save it for the tooth fairy,"
Toby tells her.
"She might even bring you a treat!"
"Wow!" Lottie says.
"I wish I had a loose tooth!" Mia adds.
Anna wobbles her tooth some more.

"Chewing gum can make
your tooth come out faster,"
Toby tells Anna.
"Maybe I have some gum."
He empties his pockets.
"Nope," he says. "Sorry!"

The twins watch Anna all day.
Mia sees Anna wiggle her tooth
in math class.

Lottie peeks at Anna
as she wobbles it
in art class.

"How's your tooth?" Lottie asks at recess.
Anna goes to wiggle it.
"I lost my tooth!" she says.
"That's **good** news," Toby says.

"No!" Anna cries. "I **really** lost it.
I don't know where it is!
Now the tooth fairy will never come!"
She bursts into tears.

"Look!" Mia points at the ground. "Glitter!"
"Oh, it's my favorite color – pink!" Lottie says.
"Maybe the tooth fairy left it for us,"
  Mia says. "Let's see where it leads!"

Lottie, Mia, and Toby
follow the trail of **glitter**.

library

gym

art room

"Do you think Anna's tooth
is in here?" Lottie asks.
They all look around the art room.
"Aha!" Mia cries, pointing up.
She sees Anna's tooth!

"Anna must have lost it
while she was gluing feathers
to her mask," Lottie says.
"That's too high for us to reach,"
Toby says.
"I'll go ask for a stool."
He runs out of the room.

Lottie and Mia share a look.
They have a VERY BIG secret.
They can help Anna
without waiting for a stool.
All they need is...

... a little twin magic!
Lottie and Mia link their pinkie fingers
and whisper a magical charm:

"**When TWINS get** *together*,

we're stronger **than ever!**

TWIN magic azam,

let's do what WE can!"

Swoosh!

A cloud of sparkling dust shimmers over the sisters. They twirl around and turn into magical Super Twins!

Mia giggles as something wiggles in her pocket.
"No need to fear! Rosie is here!"
a squeaky voice cries.
It's their magical friend, Rosie the unicorn!

"Hurry!" Lottie says.
"We need to get the tooth down
before Toby comes back."
"Rosie," Mia says,
"please watch the door."
Rosie flies over to the door.

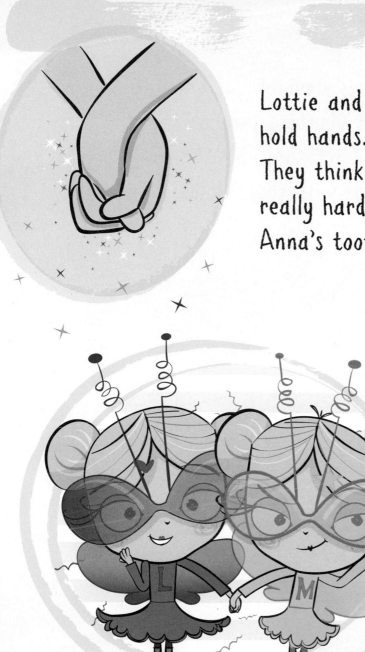

Lottie and Mia
hold hands.
They think really,
really hard about
Anna's tooth.

They feel their Super Twin magic
starting to work!

The tooth is moving!
Soon, it is floating through the air.
Together, Lottie and Mia can
move things with their minds!

"Whee!" Rosie cries as she tumbles
into a big box.
Just then, Toby runs back in the room.

He gasps. "Who are **you**?"
Toby doesn't recognize the twins
in their Super Twin outfits.
Lottie and Mia lose their focus
and the tooth falls to the floor.

"Oops!" Rosie cries.
"Sorry I wasn't watching the door."
"It's okay, Rosie," Lottie tells her.
"Lottie?" Toby says. "Is that you?"

The twins can already tell that
Toby is a good friend.
So they share their special secret.
"You're Super Twins?" he says. "Cool!"
"You can't tell anyone," Mia warns.
"I won't — I promise!" Toby says.

Anna is thrilled to get her tooth back.
"You're super friends!" she says.
Toby winks at Lottie and Mia.
"They sure are!" he says.
Lottie and Mia smile.
Their first day of school
was **definitely** super.